This Little TIGER

To Madison,
Our Little Sunshine.

This Little TIGER

illustrated by
Charr Floyd

Josh & Wendy Torres

This little tiger...

**made some shoes
out of a gator.**

This little tiger...

put a little bark into a bell.

This little tiger...

smoked a volunteer.

This little tiger...

made some beads out of a bayou bengal.

This little tiger...

**made a pillow
out of a gamecock.**

This little tiger...

rode a razorback.

This little tiger...

searched for the colonel, but he was nowhere to be found.

This little tiger...

caught a bulldawg.

This little tiger...

tamed an elephant.

And this little tiger...

yelled WAR EAGLE all the way to Jordan-Hare!

The End

About the Authors

Josh and Wendy are originally from New York and Georgia, respectively, but because o Josh's ten years of Marine Corps service, they consider many places in the southeast home They currently live in Birmingham, Alabama With the birth of their first child and their love of college football, Josh and Wendy create "This Little Tiger", and they hope others ca share their team spirit using "This Little" serie of books with their children.

To learn more about Josh and Wendy's current and future products, please visit
www.thislittlecompany.com

Have a book idea? Contact us at:
Mascot Books
P.O. Box 220157
Chantilly, VA 20153-0157
info@mascotbooks.com